# Poverty

Look for these and other books in the Lucent Overview Series:

| | |
|---|---|
| Abortion | Illegal Immigration |
| Acid Rain | Illiteracy |
| Adoption | Immigration |
| Advertising | Memory |
| Alcoholism | Mental Illness |
| Animal Rights | Money |
| Artificial Organs | Ocean Pollution |
| The Beginning of Writing | Oil Spills |
| The Brain | The Olympic Games |
| Cancer | Organ Transplants |
| Censorship | Ozone |
| Child Abuse | The Palestinian-Israeli Accord |
| Cities | Pesticides |
| The Collapse of the Soviet Union | Police Brutality |
| Dealing with Death | Population |
| Death Penalty | Poverty |
| Democracy | Prisons |
| Drug Abuse | Rainforests |
| Drugs and Sports | The Rebuilding of Bosnia |
| Drug Trafficking | Recycling |
| Eating Disorders | The Reunification of Germany |
| Elections | Schools |
| Endangered Species | Smoking |
| The End of Apartheid in South Africa | Space Exploration |
| Energy Alternatives | Special Effects in the Movies |
| Espionage | Sports in America |
| Ethnic Violence | Suicide |
| Euthanasia | Teen Alcoholism |
| Extraterrestrial Life | Teen Pregnancy |
| Family Violence | Teen Sexuality |
| Gangs | Teen Suicide |
| Garbage | The UFO Challenge |
| Gay Rights | The United Nations |
| Genetic Engineering | The U.S. Congress |
| The Greenhouse Effect | The U.S. Presidency |
| Gun Control | Vanishing Wetlands |
| Hate Groups | Vietnam |
| Hazardous Waste | World Hunger |
| The Holocaust | Zoos |
| Homeless Children | |

# Poverty

by Richard Worth

LUCENT
BOOKS

**Library of Congress Cataloging-in-Publication Data**

Worth, Richard.
    Poverty / by Richard Worth.
        p.   cm. — (Lucent overview series)
    Includes bibliographical references and index.
    Summary: Examines poverty-stricken areas and groups and
programs to alleviate poverty, including welfare.
    ISBN 1-56006-192-8   (alk. paper)
    1. Poverty—United States—Juvenile literature.   2. Poor—
United States—Juvenile literature.   3. Public welfare—United
States—Juvenile literature.   [1. Poverty.   2. Poor.   3. Public
welfare.]   I. Title.   II. Series.
HV91.W68    1997
362.5—dc21                                                96-47850
                                                               CIP
                                                                AC

# Contents

# Introduction

STUDIES OF AMERICAN presidential elections show that poor people vote in fewer numbers than do more well-to-do members of the population. One reason, experts say, is that the poor believe their vote doesn't count for much because the government does so little to help them.

This belief may be growing as a result of significant changes in welfare laws and hardening attitudes toward the needy. Welfare—a collection of state and federal programs designed to help the needy—was long considered an entitlement that the poor could receive for a lifetime. Now states are setting strict time limits on welfare benefits and forcing many poor people to go to work. Meanwhile, more communities are refusing to expand their aid to the needy, restricting panhandling by the homeless, and permitting practices that exploit poor migrant farmworkers.

All of these changes are occurring at a time when the American poverty rate is climbing. The rise has been blamed on a number of causes: the decay of large cities, the bankruptcy of many family farms across the country, a decline in the number of unskilled jobs traditionally filled by poor people, and an increasing number of single-parent families who often rely on welfare to survive. While politicians devise ways to move people off welfare and into work, there is no guarantee that work alone will eliminate the problem of poverty. Most former welfare recipients move into low-skill jobs with no health benefits and a pay rate too low to lift them above the poverty line.

The term "poverty line" is often used in discussing the poor. During the 1960s, economist Mollie Orshansky developed a method of calculating the income level below which people are defined as poor. It is still being used today. She determined that families spent approximately one-third of their income for food. Therefore, the official poverty line was defined as three times the amount it costs to buy nutritious food for a family. The current poverty line is $15,600 for a family of four people. Many working Americans, however, do not earn enough to raise their families above the poverty line. A primary reason is a low minimum wage. In 1996 Congress voted to raise the minimum wage from $4.25 per hour to $5.15 per hour. But even full-time employment at this rate would not be enough to lift a minimum wage earner and his or her family out of poverty. Secretary of Labor Robert Reich points out that these families would still need welfare benefits to reach the poverty

*As the poverty rate continues to rise in the United States, many people are forced to receive federal assistance, called welfare, in order to support themselves and their families.*

*Studies show that poor children often repeat the cycle of poverty as adults. Despite efforts to alleviate poverty, little headway has been achieved.*

line. According to the *New York Times*, Reich asserts that the impact of inflation means that the minimum wage earner is falling further and further into poverty.

Though wage earners are struggling to keep pace with the immediate effects of inflation, the children of the poor face residual problems that may lead them to repeat the cycle of poverty from which their parents cannot escape. In fact, a report by the Annie E. Casey Foundation states that the number of children of the working poor increased from 3.4 million to 5.6 million between 1974 and 1994. And, like children on welfare, these children have higher high school dropout rates and higher incidences of juvenile delinquency and teenage pregnancy, all factors associated with continued poverty in adulthood.

Are there any solutions, any methods that can break this cycle of poverty? In towns and cities across America, some programs are under way that seem to be achieving limited success. They often rely on a combination of public and private funding, community support among the poor themselves, and, above all, patience. There are no easy solutions, no magic potions that will make poverty miraculously disappear. Poverty has afflicted American society for generations; it is not likely to be eliminated in the near future.

# 1

# Faces of Poverty: Past and Present

A group of sixth graders prepares to leave for their graduation photographs. But one boy holds back. "What's the matter?" his teacher asks him softly. The boy's eyes fill with tears. "It's almost the end of the month," he says. "The welfare money has run out, so my mother can't afford to pay for a picture until the next check arrives." (Incident recorded by the author)

For over five decades, this stooped, gnarled woman has supported herself as a migrant worker picking vegetables from Florida to California. Finally, the insecticides sprayed on the plants became too much for her. "My hands would swell up every night," she says, "and I'd go to sleep clawing them." But instead of going on welfare, she began hunting for aluminum cans in trash bins and turning in the cans for money. (Jacqueline Jones, *The Dispossessed*)

In a large eastern city, soup kitchens are serving 90,000 free meals a day to the poor, [fully one-third of whom] are children. At the same time, another 50,000 are being turned away because there isn't enough money to feed them. One little girl who is fortunate enough to receive a free meal explains why she and her mother are forced to come to the kitchen. "Mama doesn't have any food," she says. It seems the refrigerator had gone bare a day earlier. (Rachel Swan, *New York Times*, December 31, 1995)

IN AMERICA TODAY, poverty wears many faces. It is a condition that can afflict anyone, of any age, in any age.

Many of the people who originally settled America were poor. They came to the New World to escape the poverty of Europe, hoping to find a better life for themselves and their children. John Rolfe, one of the early leaders of the Virginia colony and the husband of the Native American princess Pocahontas, explained:

> Too many poor tenants in England work the year around, rising early and going to bed late, living in poverty, having great difficulty paying their landlord's rent, and experiencing daily . . . worry about feeding themselves and their children. What happiness they might enjoy in Virginia.

Captain John Smith, who wrote a history of the colony, agreed with Rolfe. He believed that the colonies offered enormous opportunities for prosperity to England's poor. As Smith put it: "What man who is poor or who has only his merit to advance his fortunes can desire more contentment than to walk over and plant the land he has obtained by risking his life? . . . Here nature and liberty give us freely that which we lack or have to pay dearly for in England."

The majority of people who came to America fulfilled Smith's optimistic predictions. Some became successful farmers, some traders or shopkeepers, and some were trained as lawyers, physicians, and craftsmen. But not

*The original settlers of America fled the poverty of Europe with hopes of prosperity in the New World.*

everyone found that America was a land of great promise. There were always some who were less fortunate—women widowed without means of support, children orphaned by disease, and elderly citizens too old or too sick to work.

During the seventeenth and eighteenth centuries, towns and cities provided aid to the poor in their own homes and established almshouses, or poorhouses, to care for children and the elderly who could not live on their own. Churches and private charitable organizations also helped the poor, especially abandoned children. Many cities had orphan societies that attempted to place children in private homes and even arranged to send some of them to families in western settlements to work and enjoy the fresh air of the country.

In the nineteenth century, hundreds of thousands of immigrants left Europe to escape terrible famines in the countryside and grinding poverty in the smoky cities of the Industrial Revolution. Many of these immigrants came

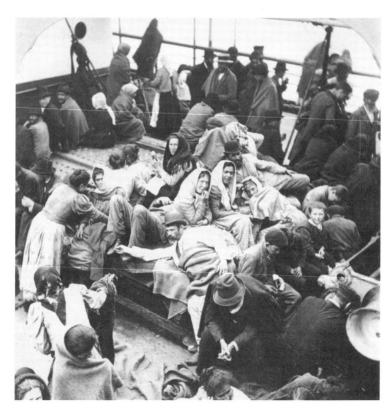

*European immigrants huddle together aboard a ship bound for America. During the nineteenth century, immigrants abandoned the famine-stricken countryside and poverty-ridden cities of Europe, setting sail for New York City.*

through Castle Garden, a large auditorium in New York City, the principal entry port for Europeans coming to America. In 1860 alone, more than one hundred thousand men, women, and children arrived, swelling the population of the city over the million mark. New York was one of the most prosperous cities in the land. Its harbor was filled with tall-masted schooners, steamboats, and large paddle wheelers; Wall Street had become the financial center of the nation; and along Broadway were fashionable stores that catered to the city's wealthiest families. Unfortunately, most immigrants would only see this part of the city at a distance, if they saw it at all.

## The urban poor in early America

As one commentator put it: "Strangers coming to New York are struck with the fact that there are but two classes in the city—the poor and the rich." The poor, which included the immigrants pouring off the ships in New York Harbor, lived in the slum sections of the city, such as Five Points and the Lower East Side. Here entire families might be crowded into a single room with no windows to provide fresh air, no indoor plumbing or clean water, and only a wood stove to produce heat in the winter. Jacob Riis, a nineteenth-century reporter and reformer, described the plight of the poor in his book *How the Other Half Lives*, which takes his readers inside a New York tenement building.

*Nineteenth-century reformer Jacob Riis captured the destitution of New York City's slums in his photographs from the late 1800s.*

> Be a little careful, please! The hall is dark and you might
> stumble over the children pitching pennies back there. . . .
> Here where the hall turns and dives into utter darkness is a
> step, and another, another. A flight of stairs. . . . Close? Yes!
> What would you have? All the fresh air that ever enters these

*Young brothers pose in their tattered clothes before photographer and social reformer Jacob Riis. In New York City during the late 1800s, children often contracted diseases like measles, tuberculosis, or scarlet fever, which were worsened by the unsanitary living conditions.*

stairs comes from the hall door that is forever slamming, and from the windows of dark bedrooms that in turn receive it from the stairs—their sole supply of the elements God meant to be free, but man deals out with such niggardly hand. That was a woman filling her pail by the hydrant you just bumped against. The sinks are in the hallway, that all the tenants may have access—and all be poisoned alike by their summer stenches. Hear the pump squeak! It is the lullaby of tenement house babes. In summer, when a thousand thirsty throats pant for a cooling drink in this block, it is worked in vain. . . . Listen! That short hacking cough, that tiny helpless wail—what do they mean? . . . Oh! A sadly familiar story. . . . The child is dying with measles. With half a chance it might have lived; but it had none.

Many children contracted diseases such as measles, tuberculosis, and scarlet fever aggravated by unsanitary living conditions. New York City attempted to deal with this problem by establishing health clinics where poor people could receive medical care and baby health stations where tenement children could obtain pure milk.

But the real problem was that people were simply too poor to afford homes where the water was clean, or to put enough healthy food on the table to feed their families properly. Many of the poor, adults as well as children, worked in factories ten to twelve hours a day for pitifully low wages. If they became sick or were injured on the job, there was no health insurance to pay for their medical bills. Some of the poor tried to support themselves by working at home. Mothers and daughters made items for sale, from clothing to artificial flowers, or did laundry and sewing for wealthier people to earn a few extra dollars. But it wasn't enough to climb out of poverty. One man who grew up in that period recalled his own experience:

"A boy stands in front of a candy store—in front, mind you. He sees a hundred varieties of sweets, but he doesn't have a penny, one cent."

## Rural poverty after the Civil War

Not all the poor lived in the cities. At the end of the Civil War, four million African Americans had been freed from slavery. Republican congressmen such as Thaddeus Stevens of Pennsylvania proposed giving each African American family forty acres of land and fifty dollars as a first step toward self-sufficiency. But no such policy was adopted. Instead, many former slaves found themselves working on the cotton plantations for their former masters. Under a system known as sharecropping, African Americans received a share of the money for the cotton crop after it was picked and sold each year. In the interim, the

*African American sharecroppers pick cotton on a southern plantation in this photograph from 1890. Although the Civil War freed African Americans from slavery, few were ever able to escape poverty.*

sharecroppers purchased food and other necessities on credit extended by plantation owners. Since the sharecroppers received very little money for their work, they tried to supplement their income by gardening, fishing, and working at odd jobs off the plantation. But very few ever escaped a life of poverty and debt.

It has been estimated that a half century after emancipation 75 percent of all black farmers were still working as sharecroppers. In addition, the so-called Jim Crow laws in the South enforced racial segregation in transportation, restaurants, and schools. Schools for African Americans were far inferior to those for white children, and at the turn of the century fully half of black children grew up illiterate, which severely hindered their efforts to obtain meaningful employment.

But African Americans were not the only people to experience rural poverty. Many southern whites were forced to scratch out a living on meager farms that barely supported their families. Others worked in coal mines, lumber mills, and textile plants where wages were low and employees' families lived in company towns set up by the owners of the mines or mills. Here the housing was often as run-down as any tenement in a large city. Workers were also forced to buy food and other items at company-owned stores at unfairly high prices. Families often bought what they needed on credit and, as their wages never quite covered what they owed, found themselves continually in debt to their employers.

With the coming of World War I, many southerners left the farms and plantations and traveled north. Manufacturing plants in cities such as Detroit, Chicago, and New York were booming because of the demand for

*In rural areas, poor people tried to support their families by putting their children to work. This photograph is of a young miner.*

*During the Great Depression, approximately 25 percent of U.S. workers lost their jobs. Families were thrown out of their homes and left destitute as the nation struggled to rebuild the economy.*

war supplies, and factory workers were needed. In *The Dispossessed*, Jacqueline Jones quotes one migrant to Chicago: "Before the North opened up with work all we could do was to move from one plantation to another in hope of finding something better."

Over the next fifty years approximately nine million people left the South for the towns and cities of the North and the Midwest. In the period following World War I, America enjoyed a period of unparalleled prosperity. By 1929 the number of poor had declined to four million from an estimated fourteen million at the turn of the century. In fact, Herbert Hoover proudly announced shortly before becoming president in 1929 that "with the policies of the last eight years we shall soon . . . be in sight of the day when poverty will be banished from the nation."

## The Great Depression and the New Deal

Unfortunately, only a year later, the nation plunged into the worst economic depression in its history. Approximately

*Men stand in line for bread during the Great Depression. Although private charities provided America's impoverished masses with food and aid, many organizations were not prepared for the sudden increase of poor citizens in their communities.*

25 percent of all working people lost their jobs. Once-prosperous managers of large industrial firms were reduced to selling apples on street corners. "Brother, can you spare a dime?" was the refrain of the decade.

Traditionally, America had relied on private charity to help the poor. And so, during the early days of the depression, appeals went out to charities such as the Red Cross to provide food baskets and clothing to the millions of people who suddenly found themselves in poverty. Major cities also tried to borrow money to finance relief efforts, but there were just too many people who needed help. Families had been thrown out of their homes because they could no longer afford to pay the monthly rents and were forced to live in makeshift communities of cardboard shacks that became known as "Hoovervilles," after President Hoover, who seemed to be doing very little to alleviate the hardships of the depression. Hoover had approved loans of millions of federal dollars to banks and insurance companies, hoping they would use the money to stimulate the economy and create more jobs. But the president opposed any direct payments to the poor to help them buy what they needed until economic conditions began to improve. Most people could not wait.

In 1932, desperate for a change in leadership, a majority of Americans voted for a new president, Franklin Delano Roosevelt, the Democratic governor of New York. Roosevelt promised a New Deal for the millions who had been thrown out of work during the depression, and at his inauguration in 1933 he told the American people: "Let me assert my belief that the only thing we have to fear is fear itself—nameless, unreasoning, unjustified terror which paralyzes needed efforts to convert retreat into advance."

Roosevelt immediately began to develop a series of short-term measures designed to put people back to work. In 1933, for example, his Civil Works Administration launched a nationwide public works programs. In New York City alone, 200,000 men were put to work improving parks and recreation areas. More massive programs followed: In announcing the Works Progress Administration in 1935, Roosevelt said, "This is a great national crusade to destroy enforced idleness which is an enemy of the human spirit generated by this depression." Over the next decade the WPA would spend $11 billion employing 8.5 million people building roads, bridges, and public buildings such as schools and post offices.

*When President Franklin Delano Roosevelt took office in 1933, his Civil Works Administration immediately began creating jobs for the nation's unemployed.*

## Social Security

One of the principal pieces of legislation passed under the New Deal was the Social Security Act of 1935. Secretary of Labor Frances Perkins predicted the unprecedented measure would "carry us a long way toward the goal of economic security for the individual." For the first time, the government was offering a safety net for Americans who suffered from poverty. The new bill included unemployment insurance for men and women who found themselves out of work, old-age benefits to retired workers, and financial aid to families

headed by widowed or divorced women. This program, called Aid to Families with Dependent Children (AFDC) was "designed as a temporary benefit to help a family through a period of crisis," according to Jill Berwick, author of *Faces of Poverty*. But in the years ahead, it would become the foundation of America's welfare system.

The programs sponsored by the New Deal put millions of Americans back to work, but they did not end the Great Depression. It was World War II that created jobs in America's factories, which had to gear up to produce guns, tanks, airplanes, and other war matériel for American soldiers. Unfortunately, these long-term jobs were not evenly distributed. African Americans still faced discrimination in hiring. A study conducted in Atlanta, for example, revealed that blacks experienced an unemployment rate nine times higher than that of whites. And too often the work African Americans obtained was limited to unskilled, lower-paying jobs. In *The Dispossessed*, Jones quotes one frustrated African American worker: "If a

*World War II was a boon to the U.S. economy; millions of Americans returned to the workforce, many as factory workers producing war matériel.*

white man and a black man walk up for an opening, and it ain't no shovel in that job, they'd give the job to the white man, but if he got an opening and there's a shovel in it, they'd give it to the black man."

After the war ended, even these unskilled jobs began to disappear as automation started changing American industry, replacing workers with machines during the decade of the 1950s. A similar transformation had been occurring in rural areas of the South: In the coal industry, labor-saving machinery was throwing miners out of work and on the cotton plantations sharecroppers were being replaced by mechanized equipment. In some areas of the Appalachian region, such as Kentucky, West Virginia, and Tennessee, unemployment skyrocketed to as much as 80 percent of the working population. During the 1950s, it was estimated that 20 percent of American families were living in poverty in cities and rural areas across the nation.

## The War on Poverty

In 1964, President Lyndon Johnson stated that an essential goal of his administration would be "an America in which every citizen shares all the opportunities of his society." This was the philosophy behind Johnson's War on Poverty, which was aimed at solving some of the chronic problems that afflicted the poor. New programs multiplied: The Job Corps was designed to provide vocational training for young people so they could obtain jobs. Head Start focused on early childhood education for preschoolers from low-income families. Public housing projects opened for the Appalachian poor and urban renewal initiatives aimed to clean up the slum areas of major cities. Medicaid made health care available for those who were too poor to afford it, and the food stamp program provided coupons to the poor redeemable for food. At the same time, existing poverty programs were expanded—AFDC, for example, was supporting more than two million families by the end of the 1960s.

Meanwhile, the American economy was expanding, and fourteen million Americans climbed above the poverty

*When companies close factories or relocate their operations, thousands of people are left without jobs. Over three million U.S. manufacturing jobs have been lost since 1979.*

line between 1959 and 1969. Nevertheless, 12 percent of the population was still considered poor.

## The new economy

During the last two decades of the twentieth century, poverty rates have been rising again. Today an estimated one-sixth of Americans living in rural areas are classified as poor, and 20 percent of the urban population live in poverty, according to *America's New War on Poverty*. Several factors have contributed to this situation, but a principal cause is the changing face of the American economy.

Since 1979, over three million domestic manufacturing jobs have been lost. Companies trying to compete in a global economy need to keep their costs as low as possible. Frequently, the wages for industrial workers are lower in the developing nations of Latin America or the Far East, so companies have moved their manufacturing operations to these parts of the world. Generally, the unskilled jobs were the first to go, which increased unemployment among African Americans who might find replacement jobs scarce. Wages have also dropped for those people who are still employed in manufacturing in the United States. Since 1973, for example, African Americans have seen their paychecks decline by 24 percent, according to a 1992 report in *Business Week*.

The disappearing manufacturing jobs have been offset by increases in lower-paying positions in service industries. This means that many people who used to work at jobs that paid $15 to $20 per hour have been forced to take jobs in fast-food restaurants or retail stores that pay only $5 to $7 per hour and don't provide any health care benefits. In one midwestern community, for example, thousands of people were laid off when a large meat packing plant closed. Many of them found jobs at nearby shopping malls, but the salaries were so low that their families suddenly experienced severe financial problems. According to *U.S. News & World Report*, between 1979 and 1992 the number of working people who have fallen into poverty has increased by 50 percent.

As people moved to follow job opportunities, America's cities began to decay. Over the past half century, many people who could afford to leave the cities have moved to suburban areas. The poor have remained behind, where they are forced to deal with inner-city problems of drugs,

*Trash litters the sidewalks of Harlem, a poverty-stricken pocket of New York City. The poor, who cannot afford to leave the inner city, face problems of drugs, crime, and unemployment.*

violence, inadequate schools, dilapidated housing, and limited employment opportunities.

Even outside the cities, unemployment has remained high in some rural areas. The War on Poverty failed to make substantial inroads into pockets of chronic poverty such as Appalachia or the Mississippi Delta. In one area of rural Maine, for example, 80 percent of the population live below the poverty line. Unemployment is also extremely high on Native American reservations. Approximately half

*Today, approximately half of the families living below the poverty line are headed by single women.*

of all Native Americans reside on these reservations, some of which report poverty levels of 40 percent, according to the *New York Times*.

## The new victims

The breakdown of the so-called nuclear family has also been blamed for increases in poverty. Today approximately half of all marriages end in divorce. Women usually receive custody of their children, while men are expected to pay child support. But almost one-third of divorced fathers pay little or nothing. And women often cannot earn enough to adequately support their families. As Congresswoman Patricia Schroeder from Colorado puts it: "There are an incredible number of women who are one man away from poverty and don't know it."

The U.S. Census Bureau reports that approximately half of the families living in poverty today are headed by single women. In some cases, their poverty follows a divorce; in others, single women are bearing children without means to support them. Each year, for example, an estimated half million teenagers give birth in America, two-thirds of whom are single. Many of these women try to survive on AFDC, which still keeps them in poverty. What's more, the actual value of the AFDC benefits plus food stamps has declined by 26 percent over the past twenty years.

Poverty reflects various social changes in America, from shifts in the economy to a breakdown of stable family values. These changes have become part of American culture and they ensure that poverty will remain a widespread problem affecting many people in all parts of the country.

# 2

# Poverty in the Cities

HARTFORD, THE CAPITAL city of Connecticut, is an example of troubled cities throughout America. As automobiles clog the outbound highways during the evening rush hour on a typical weekday, the city becomes a ghost town. Over the years, more and more residents have moved to the suburbs and the city has seen its population shrink from almost 150,000 in 1980 to approximately 125,000 today. Condominiums built during the 1980s to attract middle-class families have been abandoned. Many restaurants have been closed and shuttered, hotels have closed their doors, and retail stores have left for the suburban malls. Hartford, which is home to some of the nation's largest insurance companies, has also been hit by corporate downsizings in which thousands of people have lost their jobs. Manufacturing firms have relocated elsewhere. Unemployment in the city is well over 10 percent, nearly double the national average of 5.5 percent. And the number of residents receiving food stamps has climbed steadily during the 1990s, reaching an average monthly caseload of 20,000.

## "Poverty, Inc."

Hartford, which has long been known for its willingness to help the poor, is now dubbed by some experts "Poverty, Inc." It has become a mecca for social services throughout the region. All the AIDS residences and methadone clinics as well as the only shelter for battered women, the only centers for released convicts, and most of the homeless shelters are in Hartford.

Approximately 25 percent of the residents are on welfare, further straining a city budget that is already overburdened. Social service agencies testify that most of their clients live in Hartford, but city leaders worry that many of the poor may be moving to the city simply to take advantage of the poverty programs offered there. In 1995 the city council took the extraordinary step of saying no to any additional homeless shelters or treatment centers. "We have more than our fair share," Mayor Mike Peters told the *New York Times*. Hartford is not alone. At least thirty other cities have tried to limit services designed to help the poor. Not only do urban leaders feel that their cities are already doing enough, they also question whether expanding poverty programs is the best way to help the poor achieve self-sufficiency and higher living standards.

In related moves, cities such as New Orleans, Louisiana, and Akron, Ohio, have passed ordinances restricting panhandling, or begging, by the poor. In New Orleans a person is required to obtain a $50 license to stop motorists on the city's streets and beg for money.

*Although the population of urban Hartford, Connecticut, has drastically declined since 1980, the number of residents who receive welfare has continued to increase.*

*Some cities have passed ordinances restricting panhandling by the poor. In New Orleans, a person must obtain a $50 license before he or she can beg for money from motorists.*

These changing attitudes toward the needy come at a time when the gulf between the rich and the poor in America is widening. A *New York Times* analysis reports that during the decade of the 1980s, the incomes of the richest 1 percent almost doubled, while the poorest segment of the population experienced a decline in income of about 10 percent. Forty percent of poor Americans live in the center cities, which have become increasingly isolated islands of poverty, violence, and desolation. A majority of the impoverished are members of the working poor. They hold down low-paying jobs as file clerks in large offices, dishwashers in restaurants, janitors in high-rise hotels—jobs that pay little more than the minimum wage. As a result, they can barely afford to buy food or pay the rent on run-down apartments.

## Education in the inner city

Poor people face many obstacles when they attempt to climb out of poverty. One of the most difficult is obtaining a quality education, which is essential to finding a good job. As the National Research Council reports: "Children from affluent schools know more, stay in school longer, and end up with better jobs than children from schools that enroll mostly poor children." Experts point to a variety of reasons that may explain these differences. Wealthier schools often attract better teachers and offer more challenging courses and superior facilities. Many inner-city schools lack a sufficient number of computers to give students all the training they need to compete for jobs that demand a high level of computer skill. These schools simply don't have the money to buy them. City budgets are already stretched to the breaking point paying for welfare and crime prevention.

Another reason why poor children may be falling behind their wealthier peers, experts believe, is that affluent parents demand that their schools set very high standards for achievement. In addition, students in these schools may have more positive role models among their classmates—that is, children who are performing exceptionally

SEPARATE BUT EQUAL

well and act as pacesetters for their peers. Whatever the reasons, standardized tests reveal a tremendous performance gap between poor children and affluent children. In Bridgeport, Connecticut, for example, students routinely score twenty to forty points below children in the surrounding suburban communities on mastery tests in reading, writing, and mathematics.

The threat of violence in inner-city schools is another factor affecting students' performance. According to a Louis Harris poll conducted for the Teens, Crime, and the Community Program, approximately one-third of the respondents said they had cut school on certain days because they were afraid to go to class.

## High school dropouts

Many poor children never graduate from high school. And the unemployment rate for dropouts is 75 percent higher than that for high school graduates, according to *U.S. News & World Report.* An alarming *Business Week* report states that in Boston, for example, approximately 40 percent of students drop out of high school, and about half of those who do receive their diplomas are illiterate. This means that they are unqualified for most jobs, and usually find themselves condemned to remain in poverty.

*In affluent schools, children are able to learn valuable computer skills that will help them compete for jobs after graduation.*

*Sunset Industrial Park (pictured) in Brooklyn is one of many enterprise zones—urban areas where companies offer jobs to the poor in return for government tax breaks, loans, and reduced utility rates.*

Unfortunately, even those graduates with the credentials to seek employment often discover that no jobs exist for them in the cities. Because of factors such as crime and high taxes, many employers have left the cities for safer, cheaper locations in the suburbs or in other parts of the world. Cleveland, Ohio, for instance, has seen 37 percent of its factory jobs disappear since 1979, according to *Business Week*. And most poor people lack the money to commute to jobs in suburban areas.

During the 1980s, President Ronald Reagan tried to increase the number of inner-city jobs through the establishment of what he called enterprise zones. Companies that built plants in designated urban areas and offered jobs to the poor and disadvantaged were given substantial tax breaks. Many states developed similar programs that also included construction loans for new businesses and reduced rates for water and electricity. Although these programs may have brought some improvement to the employment picture in areas such as East Harlem, New York, studies have shown that overall the enterprise zones have not been particularly successful. Though these zones were expected to create tens of thousands of employment positions, New York State comptroller Carl McCall reports that between 1988 and 1993 a development zone in the

Bronx created only 163 new jobs while another zone in Brooklyn created only 147. According to the National Research Council, "taxes are too small a component of firm costs or even of firm profits to have much impact on location decisions." The council goes on to point out that those firms that do decide to take advantage of the tax breaks usually offer low-paying, low-skill jobs that "will not get a poor family above the poverty line."

Some employers claim reluctance to hire the poor because they may have lost the work ethic. In the Red Hook section of Brooklyn, for example, local business owners told the *Washington Post* that they are hesitant to hire the local poor because they are unreliable and don't have a strong desire to work. Instead, employers are hiring recent black and Hispanic immigrants from the Caribbean who they say are more highly educated and far more willing to put in long hours on the job. As a result, many black and Puerto Rican longtime residents of the Red Hook public housing project cannot find employment.

The South Brooklyn Development Corporation is currently trying to address this problem. For example, it has established a thrift shop where minority residents can acquire employment skills. In addition, the development corporation is providing training for the poor so they can receive bus and truck driver licenses that will qualify them for jobs with transit companies that have moved into the area. But this program can only deal with a small part of the problem.

Some experts charge that there is rampant discrimination against the African American and Hispanic poor, two-thirds of whom live in America's inner cities. They point to a study conducted by the Federal Reserve Board in the early 1990s which revealed that minority applicants were denied home loans twice as often as white applicants with the same income.

## The growing problem

Across America the story is the same: At soup kitchens and food pantries that provide free meals, the demand is growing. A study by the U.S. Conference of Mayors indicates that requests for meals increased by an average of 9 percent between 1994 and 1995, with the largest rise occurring in Trenton, Denver, and San Francisco. According to the *New York Times*, one woman on welfare who came to a soup kitchen claimed: "A week before our checks come, we're broke. I got no food at all."

Despite increases in the number of needy people served, thousands are being turned away for lack of money to care for all of them. And an increasing number of these are children, who find themselves regularly going hungry.

Many of them are also homeless. While single males used to make up the bulk of the homeless population, now an equal number of people living on the streets and in homeless shelters are families. A recent study of the homeless in New York City conducted between 1987 and 1993 revealed that a majority of these families are headed by single women, most of whom lack a high school education and recent work experience. According to the report, over 70 percent have been drug abusers or victims of physical abuse by a husband or boyfriend. The average

*As the number of homeless people increases, soup kitchens and homeless shelters lack the resources to care for all of those in need.*

age of their children was three years old; and about half of the homeless women were pregnant or had recently given birth. A majority had received no medical care during their pregnancy, and as a result their children were often born in poor health and many died in infancy.

## Homelessness

*Scholastic Update* estimates that on any night in America, seven million people are homeless, many of whom sleep in the streets, parks, subway stations, and bus terminals of the nation's cities. Most cities provide homeless shelters so these impoverished people can get off the streets. But some shelters prove to be a mixed blessing. Residents report that they are victims of theft and violence. The shelters provide very little privacy. There may be no showers available and no facilities to cook food. Children may receive very little supervision when they return to a shelter after school if their parents are out looking for work or actually employed at a part-time job.

*A homeless family finds refuge in a Philadelphia shelter. Even though some shelters are run-down and dangerous, many others help homeless families get back on their feet by offering job training, child care, and even drug counseling.*

# The Gap Between the Rich and the Poor

Source: Luxembourg Income Study.

| | The Poor | Income Gap | The Rich |
|---|---|---|---|
| Sweden | 18,829 | | 46,152 |
| Germany | 15,257 | | 51,874 |
| Canada | 13,662 | | 56,174 |
| France | 13,003 | | 44,835 |
| Italy | 12,552 | | 44,280 |
| Britian | 11,581 | | 43,933 |
| Australia | 11,512 | | 49,863 |
| **United States** | **10,923** | | **65,536** |
| Israel | 7,871 | | 33,392 |
| Ireland | 6,692 | | 27,185 |

$0　$20,00　$40,00　$60,00

Household incomes in America show a wide gap between the rich and the poor, especially when compared to other nations. This chart uses bars to show the gap between poor households with children (left end of bar) and rich households with children (right).

By contrast, some shelters provide excellent services to the families who live there. At the Gramercy Place Shelter in Los Angeles, for example, children who need it get special tutoring and the staff even helps them find a Scout troop for after-school activities. The shelter also provides job training for parents as well as drug counseling. In Seattle, Our Place Day Care, which opened in 1986, offers child-care programs for the children of homeless parents. In addition to meals and play groups, the center also provides health screenings and immunizations for the children. Unfortunately, there is only room for eighteen kids; in Seattle, approximately five hundred children reside in other shelters or live on the streets each night.

Many cities have established programs to motivate poor families to move up and out of homeless shelters. At a Family Resource Center in Connecticut, for example, a variety of services are available to help the homeless. One center client, Anna, was living at a homeless shelter with her three daughters. The center staff helped her find a place to live and provided tutoring for her children, who had been failing in school. One daughter attempted suicide and the staff obtained help for her at a psychiatric hospital and eventually enrolled her in an outpatient school program. Another client was referred to the center after she had found an apartment but had no food or furniture. The center supplied staples from their food pantry and arranged to have free furniture delivered to her home. Other services offered by the center include adult education for people who want to obtain a high school diploma, job training, and assistance in filling out job applications and writing resumés. But, like most, this center can only help a few people.

## The downward spiral

Today, poverty afflicts many people who live in America's cities. At a time when income among the poor is declining, cities are often reducing the amount of assistance they are willing to provide. Meanwhile, poor urban children seem to be receiving a lower standard of education than their peers in the suburbs. As a result, these children are typically less qualified to obtain good jobs. In addition, the number of jobs available in cities is declining because many companies have moved to suburban locations. Consequently, the poor find themselves trapped in a downward spiral from which there seems to be very little relief.

These conditions exist not only in the cities; many of the poor in rural areas also find themselves in a similar situation. They have very little opportunity to escape the cycle of poverty and obtain better jobs, better housing, or a better future for their children.

# 3

# Rural Poverty

AT HARVEST TIME in the strawberry fields of San Diego County, California, hundreds and hundreds of stooped-over migrant workers pick fruit under the hot sun. They are the poorest of America's working poor. Many migrants have recently traveled north across the Mexican border in search of agricultural jobs. Many are Mixtec Indians, from the southern Mexican state of Oaxaca. In addition to strawberries, they also harvest the yellow grapes that are dried and turned into raisins. "Raisin grape harvesting is probably one of the worst jobs you would ever want to do," Don Villarejo, a professor at the California Institute for Rural Studies in Davis, California, told the *New York Times.* "It's a job where you need a very large number of people for a very short period of time, and most employers I have spoken to prefer the Mixtecs. They work very, very hard; they don't complain."

The Mixtecs aren't the only immigrant group who work in the fields. Haitians, Guatemalans, and Salvadorans cut sugar cane in Florida or dig potatoes in North Carolina, and immigrants from the Far East pick fruit in New Jersey and New York.

## America's poorest workers

Writer Eric Schlosser believes that there may be eight hundred thousand to nine hundred thousand migrant workers in America. Some are U.S. citizens or legal residents, but many others work in the country illegally. "Migrants are among the poorest workers in the United

*Migrant workers harvest grapes in a California vineyard. Despite their hard work and arduous tasks, migrants are among the lowest paid workers in America.*

States," Schlosser adds. "The average migrant worker is a twenty-eight-year-old male born in Mexico who earns about $5,000 a year for twenty-five weeks of farm work. His life expectancy is forty-nine years." Because so many migrants are in the country illegally, they are in no position to challenge their low wages. In addition, illegal immigrants do not qualify for unemployment compensation when they are out of work or any health insurance benefits beyond acute emergency medical care.

In the 1960s Cesar Chavez and the United Farm Workers succeeded in organizing many of the migrants. Union activism led to laws guaranteeing fair wages, vacations, and health care. But over the years, Schlosser contends, California lawmakers failed to enforce these guarantees. Growers hired illegal aliens, who would work for less than the union members. This kept labor costs low and enabled California fruits and vegetables to remain competitive in a marketplace where consumers didn't want to pay high prices for what they purchased. Meanwhile, the power of the union declined. UFW membership has shrunk from sixty thousand to only five to ten thousand today.

Some migrants now find themselves working in the fields ten to twelve hours a day, with no overtime below a sixty-hour-per-week threshold, for as little as $3 per hour. After many seasons spent stooping over and picking fruit, migrants often suffer from curvature of the spine as well as other bone and muscle problems. Some also contract skin rashes from the chemicals used to treat the plants, and a few even develop blindness.

## The lure of work

Nevertheless, more and more migrants come north to work in the fields. The pay they receive in America is still higher than what they would earn at home—assuming they could even find jobs there. Many of the migrants are men, who leave their families behind and make the trek alone to the broccoli and celery fields of Santa Maria Valley, California, or the blueberry patches of New Jersey. Sometimes these men live in makeshift shantytowns where "houses" are constructed from odd pieces of wood and plastic bags. Or they may live crowded together in unheated rooms in dingy buildings which they rent for $80 per week. Others share garages rented for up to $200 per month.

Sometimes entire families work together in the fields; after a harvest in one area, they move on to another field in another state to begin the process all over again. Children younger than ten can work in the fields, although this

*Although the wages of migrant workers are extremely low by American standards, they are still considerably higher than the wages in countries like Mexico where jobs are scarce.*

*Migrants are often unable to afford adequate housing for their families. This family of eight resides in a run-down two-room house. The family lives in only one room during the cold winter months due to insufficient heating.*

practice is illegal in any other industry. As families follow the harvest, school interruptions are inevitable and many children drop out altogether. Approximately 80 percent of adult migrant workers can read only at about a fifth-grade level, maintains *America's New War on Poverty.*

In his article in the *Atlantic Monthly*, Eric Schlosser reports that the housing some families feel fortunate to find may be only a cramped apartment for which they have to pay their employer $375 per month. Employers may even charge workers for the tools they use and the water they drink. Since competition in the agricultural industry is heavy, growers try to keep costs as low as possible, and this usually means that the migrant workers are the first to suffer.

Of course, not all growers exploit the migrants; some have a reputation for fairness. Among the strawberry growers, for example, a number of companies pay good wages and do not try to work their employees unfairly. Nevertheless, some experts believe that only political action can benefit the migrant workers. In Salinas, California, for example, the Center for Community Advocacy acts as a watchdog over growers, and migrants now represent a majority of the members on the city council, where they can work for better laws. Despite these positive steps, migrants throughout America often find themselves the victims of exploitation and poverty.

## The extent of rural poverty

Migrants form a significant, but not majority, segment of the rural population who live in poverty. Approximately one-sixth of rural Americans are impoverished, according to the federal Center on Budget and Policy Priorities, 55 percent of whom are white, 32 percent are black, and 8 percent are Hispanic. Some are former farm owners who lost their homes when prices for corn and wheat dropped. Others couldn't compete with the large collective farms and were driven out of business. The agricultural workers who lost their jobs were often unable to find new ones. Many of those who could found themselves living like migrants and earning less than minimum wage.

In rural areas such as Appalachia, a drop in coal mining jobs has severely hurt the local economy. The mechanization of the coal industry has cut the number of workers in half over the past decade. As a result, many young people are leaving this region, looking for jobs elsewhere. As a character in Chris Offutt's *Kentucky Straight* says of his town: "This is a place people move away from." In some communities, homes are left empty as people leave in search of employment. And those left behind are often consigned to living on welfare. In parts of eastern Kentucky, for example, the unemployment rate is at least 30 percent. Although some areas have been able to attract industrial parks or nurture small business development, much of the region still remains extremely poor.

## Health care

Inadequate health care is another problem that afflicts the rural poor. In the makeshift communities where migrant workers live, sanitary conditions are often primitive. Many shacks have no indoor plumbing, forcing inhabitants to obtain water from community faucets and to use outhouses. At the San Andreas camp in California, notes

Eric Schlosser, the workers fell victim to an outbreak of tuberculosis worsened by crowded living conditions.

According to a 1990 study by the Center on Budget and Policy Priorities, rural Americans living in poverty are more likely to be in failing health than the urban poor. Perhaps one reason is that there are fewer physicians in rural areas, because the sparse population cannot support a medical practice.

Some counties have no physician at all, while others lack an obstetrician or pediatrician. As a result, pregnant women are likely to postpone seeing a doctor until relatively late in their pregnancy. Such factors as a woman's physical condition and proper diet are extremely important to the health of her baby, so lack of proper medical care can have a significant impact on a child's development. But women may need to travel long distances to see an obstetrician, and the poor may lack the necessary transportation.

As some areas also lack a pediatrician, children also may not receive proper health care. As the center's report states, rural residents

> are more likely to be discouraged by the amount of time required to travel for care, particularly if it results in a loss of income from hours lost at work. Also, transportation may be

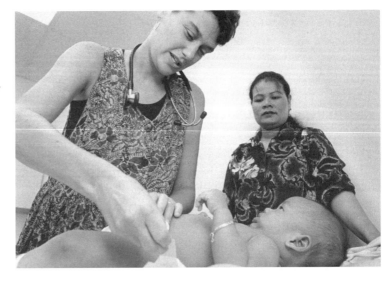

*In rural areas, the poor are less likely to receive medical attention for physical ailments. Rural communities are often unable to support a medical practice, and poor people may have difficulty finding transportation to nearby facilities.*

difficult to arrange. Public transportation is generally not available, and private transportation is often not affordable for low income households.

Not only might the poor be required to travel substantial distances for outpatient care, but hospital facilities may also be diminishing. Many rural hospitals have closed because there are not enough patients to support them and those that remain open do not offer all the specialized medical services available in city medical centers. In turn, physicians are less likely to practice in communities without a hospital in the area.

Another obstacle that prevents the rural poor from seeking adequate medical care is lack of insurance. The center report explains that nearly half of the small businesses in rural areas do not provide health insurance for their workers, as compared to about 28 percent in cities. Approximately 40 percent of farmworkers also have no health insurance.

## Medicaid

Initiated in 1965, Medicaid is financed by a combination of federal and state funds. Currently this program covers approximately thirty-seven million people. About one-half are children. The program pays for their visits to the doctor, as well as prenatal care and many other medical procedures for adults. But eligibility for Medicaid is determined by each state and fewer rural poor are covered by Medicaid than are the poor who live on welfare in the cities.

## Indian reservations

Perhaps the highest rate of poverty to be found in America today exists on the Indian reservations. Native Americans were relocated to these reservations at the end of the nineteenth century after gradually losing their lands to white settlers, backed by the U.S. Army. In 1887 Congress decided that the best way to insure Native American self-sufficiency was to allot small parcels of reservation land—160 acres, on average—to each Indian family to

*Photographed in 1898, this early Indian reservation is crowded with traditional tepees. When the U.S. government established the reservation system at the end of the nineteenth century, it hoped Native American families would live on these tracts of land and become farmers.*

live on and farm. Unfortunately, many Native Americans lacked either skill or interest in farming. For centuries, they had lived as hunters and nomads.

Some tribes, it was true, had mastered agriculture. But the small plots of land allotted by the federal government proved insufficient to support high crop yields, and many allotments were sold or leased to white settlers. During the years that followed, a majority of Native Americans living on the reservations slipped into unemployment and became wholly dependent on the federal government for financial support and social services.

In 1934, under the Indian Reorganization Act, the Roosevelt administration decided to restore a large measure of control over reservation affairs to tribal councils. But many councils seemed unequal to the task of improving the impoverished conditions that existed on many reservations. They lacked experience in self-government and were plagued by instances of corruption. President Lyndon Johnson's War on Poverty, which poured large sums of money into the reservations for such programs as education and employee training, also did little to change the lives of the Indians. Some experts maintained that the Native Americans on the reservations had become so accustomed to living on public assistance that they didn't know how to fend for themselves. Others attributed the problem to too much control by the federal government and the failure of the tribal councils.

As a result, poverty continues to be a major problem on many Indian reservations. The unemployment rate among Native Americans is three times the average for the rest of America's population and, proportionately, two and one-half times as many Native Americans live in poverty, according to *America's New War on Poverty*. Among the Navajos, unemployment reaches as high as 40 percent, and levels of 80 percent have been reported on some reservations. Indians suffer from other problems, as well. Their incidence of alcoholism and tuberculosis is five times that in the general population, seriously jeopardizing their ability to hold down jobs and escape poverty.

*Although the Indian Reorganization Act tried to remedy the impoverished conditions on reservations, Native Americans continued to live in poverty because the tribal councils were ill equipped to handle reservation affairs.*

## Tribal success stories

Despite the conditions that prevail on a number of reservations, some Indian tribes have managed to escape from poverty and become substantial success stories, due in part to effective leadership by the tribal council and an understanding of how best to use the resources that exist on Native American lands. In his book *Tribal Assets*, Robert H. White writes:

> Among these Indian lands are some of the country's most valuable resources. More than half of America's uranium, a third of its low-sulphur coal reserves, and almost a sixth of its natural gas lie under Native American soil. Indians control as much commercial forest as some of America's largest paper companies.

One group that has taken advantage of this situation is the Confederated Tribes of Warm Springs Reservation in Oregon. Native American loggers supply freshly

*Today, Indian reservations have some of the highest poverty rates in the United States. Unemployment rates for Native Americans are three times higher than the national average.*

cut trees from the reservation to a tribal-owned lumber mill, which provides jobs for hundreds of workers. Some are employed at removing the bark from the logs, others in cutting the logs into board that is sold to wood manufacturing companies, which turn it into products such as furniture. The mill also produces wood chips, which are the raw material for making paper. In addition to the mill, the Confederated Tribes also runs a sewing factory, a hydroelectric power plant, and a vacation resort. These enterprises not only provide jobs for the Native Americans of the reservation but also generate profits used to fund other projects, like programs in early childhood development and housing for the poor.

Dineh Cooperatives, Inc., a Navajo enterprise in northern Arizona and New Mexico, is another success story. Dineh owns a shopping center that provides jobs for approximately two hundred people as well as Tooh Dineh Industries, where employees manufacture precision tools and boards for computers. To the east, another tribe, the Mississippi Choctaws, operate Chahta Enterprises, which produces wire cable for the automobile industry. With the profits from this company and other businesses, the Choctaws provide job training programs for members of

using for the poor who

ed businesses on Native
ing operations, such as
*ton Post*, more than two
s currently generate $4
rican tribes annually. A
enabled Indians to open
Congress has since re-
their profits to fund so-
ly been financed by the
le such things as health
nd day care. The most
currently that of the
cut, which generates to-
day. Its Foxwoods Re-
for Native Americans as
esort has helped to revi-
of Connecticut that has
sion.

*The Foxwoods Resort on the Mashantucket Pequot reservation in Connecticut is the most successful Native American gaming operation in America. In addition to daily profits of $1 million, the expansive resort provides numerous jobs for the community and has boosted the faltering economy.*

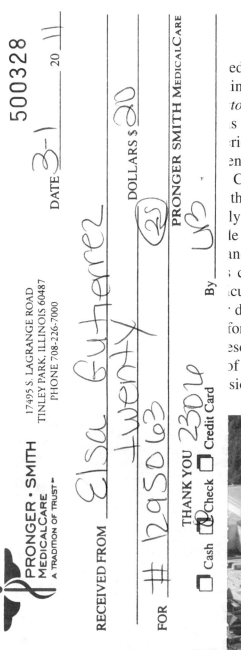

Most casinos, however, are run by independent companies based in Las Vegas and Atlantic City, not by the Native Americans themselves. And only a minority of America's two million Native Americans are currently enjoying the fruits of the gaming industry. Most reservations do not have gaming facilities. Some are too far off the beaten track to attract visitors, and some tribes, such as the Navajos and the Hopis, are morally opposed to the activity. Whether Indian gaming will prove to be a long-term solution to Native American poverty remains to be seen. But it has brought new hope to many reservations.

## Plight of the rural poor

Although some of the rural poor have been able to climb out of poverty, many others are left behind. They can't find jobs, or must work for less than the minimum wage. Adequate health care may be unobtainable, leaving adults and children unprepared for serious illness or injury. Some of the poor escape to the cities, where health care is more readily available, but adequate jobs and housing are still difficult to find. The prospects are challenging for all, but certain segments of the poor—such as single-parent families—face added responsibilities that compound the problems and make any chance to escape poverty seem unattainable.

# 4

# Single-Parent Families

CALIFORNIA CONGRESSWOMAN Lynn Woolsey made headlines when she revealed that at age thirty, the mother of three children, her husband left the family and paid no further child support. Woolsey had no choice but to apply for welfare. Even though she was working, her income left Woolsey and her children below the poverty level. "I will never forget what it was like to lie awake at night worried that one of my children would get sick or trying to decide what was more important: new shoes for my children or next week's groceries," she told the *New York Times*. "I needed welfare in order to provide my family with health care, child care and the food we needed in order to survive."

Currently, seventeen million American households are headed by single parents, most of them women. And approximately 35 percent of them live in poverty, more than twice the national average. As Jonathan Freedman writes in his book *From Cradle to Grave: The Human Face of Poverty in America*, "The prime cause of poverty in American families is the financial abandonment of children, mostly by absent fathers." Many of these men fail to support their families following a divorce.

## Independent and poor

America has the highest divorce rate in the world. One out of every two marriages ends in divorce, many of

*Many single parents rely on welfare to help pay the rent and provide food for themselves and their families. With the aid of food stamps, this young single mother can afford to buy groceries for her family.*

which involve young children. It wasn't always this way. Two centuries ago, unhappy couples stayed married for a lifetime. Past societies put a high premium on a couple staying together—no matter how unpleasant that might be—and they wrote laws that made a divorce almost impossible to obtain. Moreover, women were barred from entering many types of work, making it extremely difficult for them to support a family alone.

Conditions have changed during the late twentieth century: Millions of women have entered the workforce, and thus are less dependent on men for financial support. The legal system has also made a divorce much easier to achieve. In the past, the courts would only grant divorces on grounds such as adultery or desertion. Now, with the acceptance of so-called no-fault divorce, the court will dissolve a marriage if only one spouse wishes to end it.

From an economic standpoint, divorce often seems to benefit the parent who leaves far more than the one who remains behind and lives with the children. In one study conducted in California, reports Freedman in *Cradle to Grave*, the income of the absent parent rose by over 40 percent while that of the single parent and children declined by almost one-third. In about 90 percent of the cases, these single parents are women. And many of them fall below the poverty line following a divorce.

## Single mothers and the job market

There are several reasons why single mothers fare poorly following divorce. Some women drop out of the job market to have children. They may lose years of seniority and work experience, which makes it difficult for them to reenter the workplace and find high-paying jobs. In most fields, women have traditionally been paid less than men for the same work. Mothers with small children may also be unable to find reliable and affordable child care, so they decide to apply for welfare and stay home with their children instead of going to work. As one woman on welfare explained to *Newsweek:*

> Many times we feel, no matter how hard we try, that in some way our children are being neglected if we are holding down a job. So we stay home. We've learned that we can depend

only on ourselves. We don't enjoy living at the poverty level, but we can't see a minimum-wage job as the answer.

## Life without child support

Perhaps the major reason why so many women fall into poverty following a divorce is that so many of their former husbands don't pay child support. Only one-half of divorced fathers make full payments; the rest provide only intermittent or no support at all, according to Census Bureau statistics. In 1988 the Family Support Act required employers to garnish the wages of men who failed to make their court-ordered payments. But the law only catches a small number of delinquent fathers. Pictures of these so-called deadbeat dads have now begun appearing in newspapers. Some men have even been rounded up and thrown into jail for nonpayment. While this action forces some fathers to pay up, the majority of deadbeat dads have yet to be apprehended, leaving their children and former wives in poverty.

The United States is not alone in experiencing this problem. In Japan, for example, approximately three-fourths of divorced men are delinquent in their support payments; two-thirds of divorced men with children fall into the same category in Argentina.

"Divorce alienates men from their own families," explains Robert Bernstein, coauthor of *Divorced Dad's Handbook: 100 Questions and Answers.*

> It's often seen as an embarrassment, a magnified sense of failure, which produces pain, anger and loss of control. Divorced men often don't know how to relate to their children, because they never learned when they were married. Gradually they just drift away and fail to pay their child support payments, leaving their former wives to get along as best they can.

## The first stop for single mothers

For women and children, divorce often means a loss of economic security. Approximately 42 percent apply for welfare following a divorce, writes Jill Duerr Berrick in *Faces of Poverty.* Almost 38 percent of the women receiv-

*After a divorce, a family often experiences a loss of economic stability. Forty-two percent of these newly single parents apply for welfare.*

ing AFDC are white; 39 percent are black and nearly 17 percent are Hispanic.

Rita Henley Jensen was one of these women. Today, she is a respected journalist. But many years ago she was a young mother on welfare, following her separation from a husband who physically abused her. "Like me, many women fleeing physical abuse must make the welfare department their first stop," she explains in *Ms.* "Studies are scarce, but some recent ones of women in welfare-to-work programs across the U.S. estimate that anywhere from half to three-fourths of participants are, or have been, in abusive relationships." Women generally find welfare demeaning, and many eventually work their way off it. Seventy percent of first-time AFDC recipients have left the welfare rolls in less than two years, report David T. Ellwood and Mary Jo Bane in *Welfare Realities.*

As Jensen explains: "On welfare, I was free of the beatings [from my husband], but the assaults on my self-esteem were still frequent and powerful." She eventually went to college and graduate school. Many women somehow find

*The United States has the world's highest rate of teenage pregnancy. Every year, nearly fifty thousand girls give birth to children they are unable to support without government aid.*

a way to work, run a household, and raise their children. But the path out of poverty often proves to be extremely difficult. One woman explained to *Newsweek* that as a single mother she couldn't earn enough in a job paying minimum wage "to support even one child." This woman remained on welfare until she could get sufficient training and education to find a better job. "Fighting the low self-esteem brought on by divorce and poverty," she continued, she eventually took the "difficult step, usually without a support system, of going back to school."

## Young, single, and pregnant

About one million teenagers become pregnant each year and half of these girls give birth to their children. In 1980 nearly half of those births were illegitimate; that figure has risen to 65 percent in the 1990s, reports the *New York Times*. The rate of teenage pregnancy in the United States is the highest in the world—more than twice as high as in England or France. One reason may be that birth control is more openly discussed in these countries. In addition, abortion is often easier to obtain. In Japan, which has the lowest rate of single parenthood, a woman is stigmatized for bearing a child out of wedlock. Indeed, high schools expel students who get pregnant.

Some experts believe that Americans should take a tougher position on girls who get pregnant. They argue that the availability of welfare makes it too easy for pregnant teenagers to support themselves after the baby is born. But others disagree. Indeed, studies cited in a report by the Department of Health and Human Services point out that "welfare's role is relatively small" in accounting for illegitimate births among the poor.

AFDC is hardly enough to lift any woman and her children out of poverty. Currently in Connecticut, for example, a single woman with one child receives $705 per month. Rent alone can consume $400 of this amount, leaving very little for other necessities such as food and clothing.

If not welfare, then, what does account for these births? There is no question that some of these girls grow up in a matriarchal society—their mothers and grandmothers were single parents. Sometimes these women were married and later divorced. In other cases, they never married the fathers of their children. Many of these men may have been unemployed, or at best holding down extremely low-paying jobs, so there was no reason to look to them for support. And in most states, women can lose AFDC if their outside income exceeds specified thresholds.

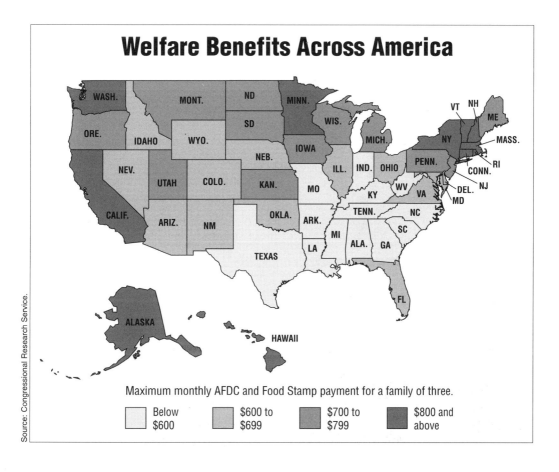

# Welfare Benefits Across America

Maximum monthly AFDC and Food Stamp payment for a family of three.

| | | | |
|---|---|---|---|
| ☐ Below $600 | ☐ $600 to $699 | ☐ $700 to $799 | ☐ $800 and above |

Source: Congressional Research Service.

Leon Dash, author of *When Children Want Children*, argues that in the impoverished culture of the inner city, pregnancy becomes a rite of passage for many girls, a way of proving they are growing up and ready to become independent of their parents. In more affluent suburbs, teenage girls can look forward to a college education and a career. These are their tickets to independence and adulthood. But many poor teenagers don't see life this way. Becoming a parent, like their mothers and their grandmothers before them, is the badge of adulthood.

## Looking for security

Studies show that approximately two-thirds of the children born to teenage girls are fathered by adult men. The inference is that girls seem to believe older men are more likely to give them security after the child is born. Unfortunately, they may be sadly mistaken. Many girls are forced to drop out of high school after having a child and approximately half never receive their diploma.

*Many teenage mothers are forced to drop out of high school. Without an education, these young mothers have difficulty finding jobs that will pay well enough to allow them to afford day care.*

In their book *Failing at Fairness*, Myra and David Sadker report the grim facts of life that confront many of these girls after they drop out. "Without education they have little hope of finding jobs that will support them and their children," the Sadkers explain, adding that the average female dropout was earning just over $3,000 annually. "More than 70 percent of single white mothers and more than 80 percent of single black mothers are raising their children in poverty."

These women usually face additional obstacles, as well. Child care is often unaffordable, so unless they can leave their children with parents or other relatives or friends, they cannot work and must depend on welfare. According to *America's New War on Poverty*, 25 percent of AFDC recipients stay in the program for more than eight years. Many of them are women who became pregnant while they were teenagers.

Young single parents also may face the added concern of having inadequate medical care for their babies. In *Faces of Poverty*, Jill Duerr Berrick describes the plight of one such parent, Sandy, who had to contend with an ill child. Sandy had been going to school and working part-time when she became pregnant. After her child was born, she intended to continue school and her job. But she lacked health insurance. When her baby became sick, she was forced to quit work and apply for AFDC so she could qualify for Medicaid.

## Programs to help teen mothers

One way to break the cycle of poverty for teens who become pregnant is to keep them in school and prevent them from having more children. Across the country, schools have established programs specifically aimed at helping teenage mothers. As Lisbeth Schorr reports in *Within Our Reach*, approximately one-third of teenagers who have one child give birth to a second before they leave adolescence. These girls are far more likely to stop attending school and rely on welfare to support themselves and their children. Therefore, many school-based programs emphasize the importance of birth control. They also help teenage girls obtain adequate prenatal care, which many teenagers are too poor to afford. Without proper care, teens are more likely to bear low-birth-weight babies who are at higher risk of illness and even premature death. Some programs try to involve a teenager's parents, since they may be the ones responsible for the child while their daughter is in school.

Keeping a teenager in school is the key element of any successful program. At Reading High, in Reading, Pennsylvania, the Once Upon a Time Child Care Center provides day care for infants while their mothers are attending school. The teenage girls take classes in science, English, and history, as well as instruction in how to care for their babies and balance the demands of being a student and a mother. The young mothers also learn effective

*This Los Angeles high school allows teenage mothers to stay in school and teaches them how to care for their children. Programs like this are instrumental in breaking the cycle of poverty by ensuring that teens graduate.*

parenting skills from the center's staff. Day care makes it possible for these girls to stay in school, graduate, and even continue their education in college, so they can eventually obtain the type of job that will enable them to support themselves and break the grip of poverty.

## Single mothers and welfare

For a single mother who is raising small children, poverty is often an everyday fact of life. Since many of these women are unskilled, their low-paying jobs often do not provide enough income to pay for food, day care, and medical care for their children. As a result, these mothers may depend on welfare, at least for a short period of time. AFDC enables them to remain at home and care for their children, and women receiving AFDC are also entitled to Medicaid as a source of health care. However, changes in the welfare laws, recently passed by Congress and state legislatures, are cutting short AFDC benefits and creating a new set of challenges for single-parent families and the poor in general.

# 5

# The Welfare Debate

IN A SURVEY released in 1996 by the Public Agenda
Foundation, a large majority of Americans say they believe the welfare system is seriously mismanaged and
needs to be changed. What changes do they suggest? They
think that people on welfare should participate in education and job training programs so they can go to work; that
child care should be available for single mothers so they
can finish school and hold down jobs; and finally, that
mothers on welfare who give birth to more children
should not have their benefits increased.

These suggestions reflect the issues that lie at the center
of a fierce debate between Republican and Democratic
lawmakers in Washington over the future of the welfare
system. Republicans believe that the federal government
will never be able to cut costs and balance its budget unless welfare spending is reduced. While Democrats generally agree, they want to achieve this goal differently.

## Block grants

Most Republicans believe that the states should have
much more control over their own welfare programs. At
present, these programs are jointly administered and
funded by state and federal bureaucrats. Republicans
would prefer that states be given block grants for welfare
with wide discretion over how to use them. This, they argue, would reduce bureaucratic red tape in Washington
and let those closest to the problem—welfare administra-
tors in the individual states—decide what works best.

Republicans conclude that the states would thus be able to operate with less money from Washington. Republican lawmakers would also impose major changes on the welfare system, including a five-year limit to the cash payments that any family could receive. This means that the main welfare program, Aid to Families with Dependent Children, previously open-ended, would be limited. Currently, this program serves about five million families at a cost of $23 billion annually. Republicans would also mandate that most adults receiving AFDC be required to work after two years and give up their benefits. In addition, the amount of food stamps that twenty-seven million Americans currently receive would be reduced. Another major change would affect Medicaid, the health care program for the poor. Fewer children and adults would be covered by the program, and the states would have much wider discretion over which health benefits they would receive. This and other changes are designed to slow the growth of Medicaid spending by $163 billion over the next seven years.

While Democrats generally agree that states should have more control over welfare and that costs must be cut, they believe that the Republicans have gone too far. "It rips at the safety net, tears it to shreds," argues Senator Frank Lautenberg, Democrat, of New Jersey. President Bill Clinton agrees, saying that the Republican plan includes "deep cuts that are tough on children." Marian Wright Edelman, head of the Children's Defense Fund, a nonprofit advocacy group for children, states that the Republican approach would "leave many children poorer, hungrier, sicker and at greater risk of abuse and neglect."

Although Democrats favor more state control over welfare, they would keep central direction of the program where it is—in Washington—fearing that states might not always administer the block grants properly. They also oppose such deep cuts in Medicaid, and would not summarily remove people from welfare if they hadn't found jobs after two years. People who were at least trying to find jobs would still receive benefits.

*Welfare recipients and their supporters protest changes to the welfare system in Washington, D.C. Critics of welfare reform argue that welfare cuts would be detrimental to the nation's poor.*

In the summer of 1996, Democrats and Republicans finally agreed on a compromise bill that was signed by President Clinton. The law is expected to save $55 billion in welfare over six years. The president said he was signing the bill "first and foremost, because the current system is broken." The new law establishes a limit of five years for welfare payments to any family. This eliminates the guarantee of lifetime welfare benefits that existed in the past. Under the new law, most adults on welfare are also required to work within two years or lose benefits. Food stamps are being cut by $24 billion over six years. In addition, welfare will now be administered by the states, which will receive block grants from the federal government along with substantial leeway for running their own programs.

## States in the driver's seat

While Washington lawmakers debated the future of welfare, many states were already making changes in the welfare system. One of the advantages of our federal system is the division of authority between a central government in Washington and fifty state governments. This enables individual states to experiment with new approaches to problems such as welfare. If an experiment works, it can be adopted by other states, and eventually by the entire country.

Under waivers, granted by the Clinton administration, state legislatures have been permitted to modify the welfare laws. A majority, for example, now impose a time limit on benefits for people who are deemed able to work but do not obtain jobs, and deny additional benefits to single mothers who have more children while on welfare.

Wisconsin has been a leader in welfare reform. Led by Republican governor Tommy G. Thompson, state laws began to change as early as 1988. In that year, the state imposed Learnfare, a program under which a family's welfare benefits were cut if a teenager had too many unexcused absences from school. While this program saved the state money and improved attendance for some students, many others seemed to ignore the law and their attendance

*In an effort to reform the welfare system, legislators passed a law that limited the amount of time a family could receive welfare payments to five years. The law also required adult family members to obtain jobs within two years of going on AFDC.*

continued to decline. In an effort to move people off welfare and into work, Wisconsin provided job training and up to twenty months of free day care so poor parents could attend the training programs.

## The two-year limit

The state is also experimenting with a program to force AFDC recipients into jobs in two years. Thus, welfare would no longer be an entitlement—that is, a poor family would not automatically be entitled to receive welfare for the rest of their lives. AFDC would have a strict time limit. Once off welfare, those who obtain employment would receive a year's worth of free health care and child care to ease the transition into the job market. Studies show that 30 to 40 percent of people who leave welfare rolls return to welfare after a year because their jobs are low-paying and provide no health benefits. In addition, many who have been living on welfare for a lengthy period of time seem to lack the attitudes necessary to hold down a job, according to *U.S. News & World Report*. Some habitually arrive for work late. Others may go to work for a while, then call in to their employer with excuses for not showing up, and eventually lose their jobs.

Another state that has been experimenting with welfare reform is Michigan. In 1991, for example, Republican governor John Engler eliminated payments to eighty thousand single adults who were receiving welfare. The short-term effect was an immediate reduction in the state's welfare costs, and approximately 20 percent of the former welfare recipients found jobs, according to the *New York Times*. But there were offsetting negative effects. According to a study conducted by the University of Michigan School of Social Work, the number of homeless people in Detroit rose noticeably, in part because of the reduction in welfare payments. The homeless adults could no longer afford the cheap rooms in single-room-occupancy hotels where they used to live. Homeless shelters were forced to increase the number of poor people they served. And much of the funding for expanding these services came from the state of Michigan. Thus, to some extent state costs were simply shifted from welfare benefits to shelters for the homeless.

*Many critics fear that welfare cuts will increase the number of homeless people, placing an increased burden on homeless shelters and charities.*

Michigan also sponsors job clubs for welfare recipients. The job club aims to shore up their self-confidence and

teaches them how to fill out job applications and write a resumé. However, some welfare recipients refuse to show up for job training although Michigan mandates that, by not attending the program, their benefits will be cut by $100 per month. In California, which has one of the most effective job training programs, results have also been mixed. Fewer than half of the people who joined the program found jobs; of these, many were still receiving some welfare benefits to supplement their low incomes. Less than 25 percent had completely left welfare for work. The state also discovered that the welfare-to-work program was costing taxpayers an average of $4,500 per person—a very high price tag.

In Connecticut, AFDC recipients have been given twenty-one months to find a job and leave welfare. The state estimates that forty thousand of fifty-nine thousand AFDC recipients will move off the rolls. Some are permitted to continue receiving aid because they are disabled or have disabled children. In a program called Jobs First in Milford, Connecticut, women who have been accustomed to receiving welfare learn how to cope with the fears they experience about going on job interviews and holding down full-time positions. As coordinator Kelley Caudle, a former welfare mom herself, tells participants: "If you don't feel good about yourself, you're going to beat up on yourself and others. But you want to be happy, feel successful and enjoy your life." Caudle believes that the best way for women to feel successful is by working, and many of the women in the program agree.

## Roadblocks

But the road out of welfare is not an easy one. Job training may only provide the most fundamental skills for low-paying, entry-level positions. Studies of three successful welfare-to-work programs in Atlanta, Georgia; Grand Rapids, Michigan; and Riverside, California, show that while earnings of participants increased by 26 percent, they were still very low. And over 50 percent of the people in these programs were still not working after two years.

Moreover, there is no guarantee that an entry-level job will inevitably lead to a more lucrative one. A study by the Brookings Institution of former welfare recipients who had gone to work between 1979 and 1990 showed that their wages over this period had risen only about six cents per hour. The process of moving people off welfare and into work that will support them is, therefore, extremely difficult.

## Changes in Medicaid

While states have been overhauling the welfare system, changes have also been occurring in Medicaid. Escalating costs for Medicaid, currently estimated at $156 billion annually, have threatened to bankrupt state budgets, forcing governors to look for other means to fund health care for the poor. Twelve states are already experimenting with new health care programs, among them Tennessee. Beginning in 1993, the state adopted a new managed care program, TennCare, which has already saved $1 billion while apparently maintaining the quality of care, according to the *Washington Post*. Under managed care, the state works with private companies that contract with doctors and hospitals to treat patients. These companies are given a fixed amount of money by the state to care for each patient, an amount that is less than the expenditures under Medicaid.

The private companies keep costs down by such means as reducing hospital stays, using generic drugs instead of more expensive brand names, and limiting patient visits to specialists, who tend to charge more than family doctors. In Tennessee, the program has saved enough money to extend health care coverage to an additional four hundred thousand people, many of them working poor who were not covered by health insurance. While TennCare is free to Medicaid recipients, the working poor must pay moderate monthly charges. As David Brown of the *Washington Post* explains, "In strategy if not in detail, TennCare is where Medicaid is headed."

## The future of welfare

With the passage of the new welfare bill by Congress, the trend toward greater state control over the system has gained impetus. "I'm totally comfortable with the states' ability to handle it," says Governor Thompson of Wisconsin. And many other governors seem to agree. Can the

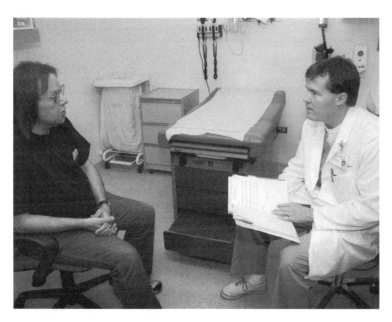

*In Tennessee, a new managed care program called TennCare was introduced as an alternative to Medicaid. Since its creation in 1993, TennCare has saved the state $1 billion.*

states run more effective, less expensive welfare programs? Will they avoid the charges of waste and corruption that have often been leveled at the current system?

Under the terms of the 1988 Family Support Act, states were supposed to reduce welfare payments to teenage mothers who failed to attend school. However, many states never enforced the law because they didn't want to spend the extra money it would take to provide child care for these mothers while they were in the classroom. This suggests that the effectiveness of welfare programs will probably vary from state to state. One state that did enforce the Family Support Act was Ohio, which cut $124 from a teenage mother's welfare check if she didn't go to school. As a result, the number of women graduating increased by 24 percent and those who found jobs jumped by 40 percent, according to *Business Week.*

Already states such as Michigan, Wisconsin, Connecticut, and California are making extensive efforts to move more people into jobs and reduce the cost of the welfare system. While the welfare rolls have been reduced, the success of these programs has been mixed. Some leave welfare and stay off it. Others are forced off welfare only

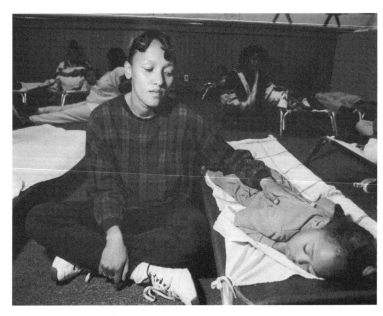

*At the Family School in San Francisco, single welfare mothers study for their GEDs, receive job training, and attend parenting workshops (pictured). Unfortunately, welfare-to-work programs like this one have had only partial success in moving people off the welfare rolls.*

to move to homeless shelters which are funded by the state. Still others seem capable of holding down a job temporarily but after a short time return to welfare again.

Some experts also point out that the low-wage, unskilled jobs that former welfare recipients obtain are the first to be eliminated in a recession. An economic downturn would thus force more people back onto the welfare rolls at the same time Washington is trimming state funds. That's the reason why governors like Evan Bayh of Indiana believe that plans to reduce federal welfare funding will be detrimental to the states. "Congress simply wants to shift the burden of the deficit to state and local government," Bayh warns.

## Relying on charity

What happens if the states cannot shoulder this burden? The hope is that private charities will step in and take on a greater share of assistance to the poor. As Speaker of the House Newt Gingrich puts it: "I believe in a social safety net, but I think it's better done by churches and by synagogues and by volunteers."

What's often overlooked, however, is that charitable organizations receive an average of 30 percent of their funding from government sources. An organization like Jewish Family Services of Los Angeles, for example, relies on government funding to help support a homeless shelter, provide tutoring for poor children, offer job counseling for the unemployed, and treat drug and alcohol abuse. In 1994 an estimated 63 percent of the budget for Catholic Charities USA came from the government. The fact is that federal, state, and local governments work through nonprofit charitable organizations to provide services for the poor in every part of the country.

If government funds are suddenly cut, how will these charities make up the difference? The obvious answer, of course, is an increase in private donations. But according to a study conducted by Giving USA, contributions to those charities that help the poor declined by 6 percent from 1993 to 1994. A decline in charitable giving combined

*The Salvation Army is just one of many charitable organizations that provide aid to poor people. Many people are concerned that government cuts will force many private charities to close their doors to the poor.*

with a reduction in government funding for welfare may prove extremely harsh on poor people.

## Abusing the system

Nevertheless, critics of the current system point out that costs have skyrocketed out of control and that some of those receiving welfare checks really aren't entitled to them. In 1975, for example, Congress enacted the Earned Income Tax Credit, at a cost of $252 million, to offset poor workers' income taxes. Since that time, the program has ballooned to $20 billion, and studies show that as much as one-third of the money may be going to workers who aren't entitled to it. Examples of abuse no doubt exist throughout the welfare system. During the 1970s, a favorite target of Republicans like Ronald Reagan was the so-called welfare queens who were collecting checks every month while they drove around in Cadillacs. But much of this abuse has been eliminated by tighter federal controls that have reduced errors and fraud from approximately 17 percent in the 1970s to an overall rate of 5 percent in the 1990s, according to *U.S. News & World Report*.

Many Democrats fear that if the states assume greater control over the welfare system, the rate of abuse and mismanagement may begin to increase again. In the past, a few states receiving block grants from the federal government have misused the money. According to an article in *Business Week*, some federal money earmarked for child care for the poor in Mississippi was used by the Department of Human Services "to buy items such as $37.50 designer salt-and-pepper shakers, as well as $40,000 in improvements to a building the state didn't own." And *U.S. News & World Report* points out that block grants from the Department of Housing and Urban Development designated for low-income housing have been diverted to such things as bringing a hockey team to a city in New York and financing off-track betting on a California Indian reservation. These isolated incidents nevertheless suggest that problems can arise in some states if they are given too much control over block grants.

## Meeting the needs of the poor

Although states and cities contend that they are closer to the poor and, therefore, know how to meet their needs better, there is no guarantee that these needs will actually be met. Abuse and corruption can exist at any level of government. Nor has any welfare program yet designed achieved a high degree of success at lifting people out of poverty. As Republican senator William V. Roth of Rhode

*Despite claims of abuse and corruption, the welfare system is an indispensable part of many people's lives. Critics hope that reform will allow the system to continue to improve conditions across the country.*

Island puts it: "Despite having spent over 5 trillion dollars in the last 30 years, the welfare system is a catastrophic failure." This may be an exaggeration. Welfare has helped some people survive until they could find jobs and support themselves, never to return to the welfare rolls again. For many others, however, the story is quite different. They seem to go back and forth from low-paying jobs to welfare. Some have never known life without it.

Any improvement in this situation is likely to be gradual and difficult. It will require a change of attitude among the poor themselves, many of whom lack the self-confidence, the skills, or the proper work habits necessary to hold down jobs. It will also require a change of attitude among American taxpayers, reluctant to admit the fact that providing training for the poor, adequate child care, and jobs sufficient to lift people out of poverty will cost untold billions of dollars. There are no quick fixes or magic cures, only years of effort and experimentation to find out what will work successfully.

# 6

# Programs That Make
# a Difference

IN THE SANDTOWN-WINCHESTER neighborhood of Baltimore, Maryland, during the 1980s, the statistics told a grim tale. Among a resident population of approximately ten thousand, half the families lived below the poverty line; 40 percent of the residents depended on welfare to survive; almost 30 percent of the new babies each year were born to single, teenage mothers; and the rate of AIDS infection was the fourth highest in the state. This could have been just another story of urban decay. But it isn't, because the people who live in this neighborhood decided to change things.

In 1990, they initiated a program called Community Building in Partnership, one of many programs involving poor people that are having an impact on poverty. That partnership involved funding from the Enterprise Institute, a nonprofit organization involved in revitalization projects throughout America. It also received funding from the city of Baltimore, whose mayor, Kurt L. Schmoke, has dedicated himself to improving neighborhoods like Sandtown-Winchester. But most important was the commitment of the people themselves to transform the entire area.

Consider, for example, community health workers Vicki Blackwell, Monica McArthur, and Torey Reynolds. They go from house to house explaining to residents how they can reduce their blood pressure by simple measures such as controlling their diets or giving up cigarette smoking. This is only a small part of an overall effort aimed at improving the health of everyone in the Sandtown-Winchester community. An organization called Healthy Start, the largest employer in the neighborhood, has trained people as nutritionists and health advocates. Healthy Start also runs a family planning clinic, and it has been instrumental in reducing infant mortality rates, which are very high in an area where a third of the people lack health insurance. Local hospitals have stepped into this breach by committing themselves to provide prenatal care for expectant mothers, pediatric care for children, and regular medical treatment for all adults free of charge, if patients are unable to afford it. At elementary schools in Sandtown-Winchester, wellness centers have been opened that offer such routine medical services as regular physicals and immunizations against childhood diseases.

Improved health care is not the only area where improvements are under way. The Home Instruction Program for Preschool Youngsters teaches young mothers how to enrich the lives of their children through games, storytelling, and other activities aimed at increasing the likelihood of success in school. Parents have also held fund-raising events to support a new Pop Warner Football League for youngsters ages seven to nine.

## Reclaiming the neighborhood

Perhaps the most striking transformation in Sandtown-Winchester has been in the physical appearance of the neighborhood. Residents have reclaimed abandoned lots and turned them into vegetable gardens. Dilapidated buildings have been completely renovated, and new homes have been constructed. Approximately six hundred have been made available at low prices that residents can afford. New home buyers also work with organizations such as Habitat for Humanity, a group that enlists the support of private citizens, including such notables as former president Jimmy Carter, in an effort to build affordable housing in towns and cities across the country. Working with these volunteers, new homeowners contribute three hundred hours to the construction of their homes.

*Former president Jimmy Carter and his wife, Rosalyn, work side by side as volunteers for Habitat for Humanity, an organization that builds affordable homes for the poor.*

While the Sandtown-Winchester program has already scored some successes, residents would be the first to admit that there is still much left to do. Many buildings await renovation, and more jobs are needed for the unemployed. Some community leaders also fear that drugs may undermine all their efforts by presenting young people with an easy method of making money and escaping their problems. "If we could just get rid of the drugs," urges Ms. Cleander Warren, "the touting, the selling, the influencing of kids to sell and use them."

## YouthBuild

One of the organizations involved in revitalizing Sandtown-Winchester is YouthBuild USA. Enrolled in the program are young people who have dropped out of school and can't find jobs because they lack basic skills. YouthBuild not only enables them to earn a high school diploma, but provides on-the-job training in building construction. One single mother, for example, wanted to be trained as a plumber; another high school dropout joined YouthBuild to become an apprentice electrician. As Youth-

*First Lady Hillary Rodham Clinton listens to a YouthBuild volunteer during a visit to Philadelphia. YouthBuild helps high school dropouts earn diplomas and gain valuable job training in the construction field.*

Build member Elsie Flores puts it, the program has "taught me to be true to myself and what I believe in and that I can be whatever I want to be. But I can't get there by doing nothing."

YouthBuild challenges its members to work hard if they want to achieve something. Aside from the project in Baltimore, YouthBuild has been engaged in rehabilitating buildings in cities such as San Francisco; Boston; Portland, Maine; and St. Louis, Missouri. As YouthBuild's St. Louis director told *Historic Preservation* magazine, "Working with their hands and building something creates a sense of accomplishment that contributes to self esteem. People who may not have been very successful in school can learn how very successful they can be." On completion of the program, young people generally find jobs in the construction industry that pay far more than minimum wage and enable them to climb out of poverty.

## City Year

Another promising project, similar to YouthBuild, is City Year. It brings together young people from various backgrounds—poor youths from urban neighborhoods as well as middle-class youngsters from the suburbs—who want to volunteer their time to improve America's cities. As part of City Year, members might run a recreation program for the elderly, renovate homeless shelters, and plant gardens in abandoned city lots. An intensive academic program is available for young people who have not graduated from high school so they can earn a diploma, and career counseling helps them find jobs. While participating in City Year, each person receives a small salary; at the end of the program they are given financial aid to continue their education or enroll in job training.

Founded in 1988 by Digital Equipment Corporation and the Timberland Company, City Year eventually became part of the AmeriCorps program. This is an effort initiated by the Clinton administration in which young people pledge a year of national service to the community in return for a small salary and a substantial payment at year's end to be used for additional education.

## Job Corps

A much older government-sponsored program aimed at helping young people is the Job Corps. Founded during the 1960s as part of President Lyndon Johnson's War on Poverty, the Job Corps primarily serves poor high school dropouts. Most live at Job Corps centers for a period of six months, exposed to a mixed curriculum of academic courses and career training. Young people examine a variety of job options—such as carpentry, computer science, food service, and health care—and with the help of staff counselors they select the career that seems most suitable to them and receive hands-on training in it. There are classes in how to fill out job applications and locate positions of employment. Counselors help students put together individualized plans with cash bonuses to mark their achievements. Students also learn how to improve social skills that are essential to career success, like conflict resolution and teamwork.

Upon completing the program, over 60 percent of the students obtain jobs. The cost of training is admittedly high, but estimates are that every dollar spent returns $1.46 in reduced welfare and other expenditures necessary to maintain people who are unemployed.

One segment of the economy predicting steady employment in the years ahead is the automobile industry. A study by the University of Michigan predicts that by the year 2003, the car companies will hire 170,000 new workers. These are good jobs, paying an average of $25,000 to $46,000, which is far above the poverty line. An organization that is training people to qualify for these jobs is Focus Hope. Each year, it takes 1,000 inner-city youths from Detroit—many of whom have dropped out of high school—and puts them through a rigorous program of academic courses and job training. Students are expected to

*A young woman studies algebra in her dorm room at a Job Corps center. The Job Corps helps disadvantaged young people receive an education while learning a vocational trade.*

*President Bill Clinton praises a trainee from Focus Hope, a group that annually trains one thousand inner-city youths for jobs in the high-tech automobile industry.*

master computer skills, which are essential for anyone working on the assembly line, and they receive hands-on training in running lathes and grinders in a machine shop. For young people who have not been used to holding a job, the program emphasizes positive attitudes toward work—including self-discipline and promptness, skills critical to keeping a good job and staying out of poverty.

## Delta Service Corps

Programs aimed at combating poverty are under way not only in America's cities but in rural areas, as well. "The Delta Service Corps has given me the chance to do what I enjoy . . . helping and meeting others," explains Ina Rouse. Ms. Rouse runs a thrift store in north central Arkansas that receives items such as clothing and furniture and distributes them to the poor. Twenty-eight volunteers participate in the program, one of many that the Service Corps runs in Arkansas, Louisiana, and Mississippi. Volunteers sign up for a year of service, participate in intensive training programs, and work together on

*Migrant farmworkers take a break from harvesting tobacco leaves on a North Carolina farm. The Farmworker Justice Fund works to improve working conditions for migrants and to protect them from the harmful pesticides that are often used in agriculture.*

teams led by people such as Ms. Rouse. Their work may involve running a food pantry that distributes meals to the poor, running child care programs that enable poor women to work, and tutoring children. "I enjoy working with students because they have so many needs," says Johnnie Ingram, who tutors youngsters as part of an ESL (English as a Second Language) program.

## Farmworker Justice Fund

Another organization aimed at helping the rural poor is the Farmworker Justice Fund, which is committed to improving conditions among migrant farmworkers. Through the efforts of this nonprofit organization, the federal Occupational Safety and Health Administration now requires large agricultural companies to provide pure drinking water, toilets, and water for washing to migrant field-workers. Tighter regulations have also been enacted to reduce the harmful effects of pesticides on farmworkers; and successful court action by the Farmworker Justice Fund has led to increased wages for some migrants.

A special program undertaken by the fund is the Farmworker Women's Health Project. Hazel Filoxsian, a member of the project, explains: "As women of color, we are a minority, and that is the first strike against us. And as farmworker women, that is the second strike against us. The first thing we need to do is to share with our sisters that this is not what we deserve in life. [We] deserve the absolute best."

At conferences, women farmworkers can discuss issues of concern to all. One of these is sexual harassment from crew leaders and men farmworkers. Another problem is AIDS, estimated to be more prevalent among migrants than the national average. Some of the women attending these conferences work in migrant health centers that serve poor farmworkers. And the information they receive can then be disseminated to their clients. The health conferences also give women an opportunity to meet with members of Congress who are active in the effort to safeguard farmworkers and talk to them about problems such as better health care, housing, and education for migrant families.

## PrairieFire

Another organization that deals with the plight of the rural poor is PrairieFire. Each year thousands of small farmers lose their livelihoods as a result of falling food prices, droughts, floods, or other natural disasters. In 1988 PrairieFire published *No Place to Be, Farm and Rural Poverty in America*. This book spotlighted the problems faced by people forced off the land who found themselves hungry and homeless. In Iowa, where the organization is based, PrairieFire secured passage of a new homestead act that made it easier for farmers who lost their land due to bank foreclosure to obtain new farms. The organization has also established a rural crisis hotline to provide advice and support for farmers facing serious financial pressures.

PrairieFire has reached out to other groups concerned about the future of small family farms. Together with religious and political leaders the organization has tried to

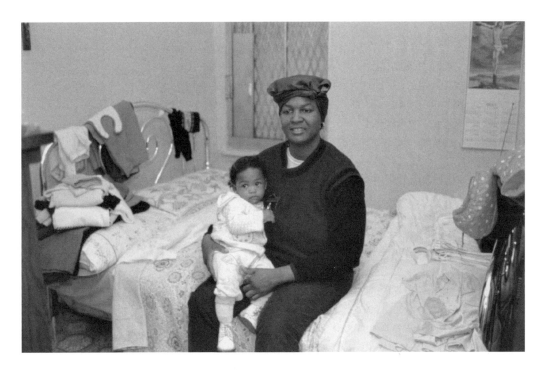

*Many organizations and charities across the country offer shelter and aid to homeless individuals and families. With help, some people are able to climb out of poverty and become self-sufficient.*

prevent the domination of food production by huge corporations, thus preserving the position of the small farmer. PrairieFire has also worked to protect the rights of immigrant workers in the meatpacking industry.

## The poor and their families

Many of the programs involving the poor are designed to help families get on their feet and become self-sufficient. One example is Families First in Atlanta, Georgia. Among their many services is a Family Development Center, which provides a homeless mother and her children with a place to live for up to a year. During this time, women can receive assistance in obtaining a high school diploma, career training, and job searches. While women are engaged in these activities, the center provides day care services for their children. Forty percent of the women are employed when they leave the facility.

In Washington, D.C., the Coalition for the Homeless also maintains shelters for families as part of its wide-ranging programs aimed at serving homeless people. Families can receive help in the coalition's emergency shelter, which offers programs to help parents deal with substance abuse, a common problem that afflicts many of the homeless. Children can also participate in a tutoring program to assist them with schoolwork. Often their education suffers as they try to cope with family upheaval caused by poverty and homelessness. Following a short stay in the emergency shelter, families can move into transitional apartments where parents receive help from employment development specialists in writing resumés, filling out job applications, and finding work.

The coalition, which serves more than three thousand homeless people annually, also maintains shelters and transitional housing for single men. There they can receive substance abuse counseling to help them remain drug free so they can hold down steady jobs as well as assistance in seeking employment so they can become self-supporting. Bobby Wade, one of the people who benefited from this program and found a job, explains that "Plenty of sessions with the social worker, substance abuse counselor, and fellow addicts and alcoholics helped me realize that I could never use drugs again."

Across America a variety of self-help programs urge the poor, working together with an array of community resources, to become self-sufficient. For many Americans, poverty does not need to last a lifetime. Nor is welfare the only method of helping the poor. While some may be unable to work because of physical or emotional problems that overwhelm them, many others are prepared to seize the opportunity to support themselves. What they often need is help—job training, education, substance abuse counseling, child care, low-income housing, health care, and a fair wage every year. Indeed, a large number of the poor are already demonstrating that with this kind of help they can become self-sufficient.

# Organizations to Contact

The following organizations are concerned with issues discussed in this book. Most have publications or information available for interested readers. Because this list was compiled on the date of writing of the present volume, names, addresses, and phone numbers may have changed. Allow as much time as possible: Many organizations take several weeks or longer to respond to inquiries.

**City Year**
285 Columbus Ave.
Boston, MA 02210
(617) 927-2500

A program that brings together young people of various backgrounds who want to volunteer their time to improve America's cities.

**The Coalition for the Homeless**
1234 Massachusetts Ave. NW
Washington, D.C. 20005
(202) 347-8870

An organization that provides a full range of programs for the homeless.

**Community Building in Partnership**
1137 N. Gilmor St.
Baltimore, MD 21217
(410) 728-8607

A program in Baltimore in which the poor work with the city and private foundations to improve impoverished neighborhoods.

### Delta Service Corps
PO Box 2990
West Memphis, AR 72303
(501) 735-4373

An organization in Arkansas, Louisiana, and Mississippi that enables volunteers to devote a year of service to helping the poor.

### Families First
1105 W. Peachtree St. NE
PO Box 7948, Station C
Atlanta, GA 30357
(404) 853-2800

An organization providing a variety of services aimed at helping poor women and their families.

### Farmworker Justice Fund
1111 19th St. NW, Suite 1000
Washington, D.C. 20036
(202) 776-1757

An advocacy group committed to improving conditions among migrant farmworkers.

### Job Corps
U.S. Department of Labor
Employment and Training Administration
200 Constitution Ave. NW
Washington, D.C. 20210
(800) 733-JOBS

A program sponsored by the federal government designed to help poor high school dropouts obtain career training.

**PrairieFire**
550 Eleventh St.
Des Moines, IA 50309
(515) 244-5671

A rural organization that helps small farmers.


**YouthBuild USA**
58 Day St.
Somerville, MA 02144
(617) 623-9900

An organization that offers high school dropouts on-the-job training in building construction.

# Suggestions for Further Reading

Suzanne M. Coil, *The Poor in America*. New York: Messner, 1989.

Karen O'Connor, *Homeless Children*. San Diego: Lucent, 1989.

Richard Worth, *Single Parent Families*. New York: Watts, 1992.

# Works Consulted

Elijah Anderson, "The Code of the Streets," *Atlantic Monthly*, May 1994.

Terry Anderson, *Sovereign Nations or Reservations? An Economic History of American Indians*. San Francisco: Pacific Institute for Public Policy, 1995.

Robert Bernstein and Richard Worth, *Divorced Dad's Handbook: 100 Questions and Answers*. Tempe, AZ: Blue Bird, 1995.

Jill Duerr Berrick, *Faces of Poverty*. New York: Oxford University Press, 1995.

Leon Dash, *When Children Want Children*. New York: William Morrow, 1989.

Jason DeParle, "Less Is More: Faith and Facts in Welfare Reform," *New York Times*, December 3, 1995.

Howard Fineman, "The New Crime Wave," *U.S. News & World Report*, August 29, 1994.

Jonathan Freedman, *From Cradle to Grave: The Human Face of American Poverty*. Atheneum: New York, 1993.

Allen Freeman, "We Need Love, We Need Support, We Need Skills . . .," *Historic Preservation*, May/June 1993.

Malcolm Gladwell, "On the Waterfront, a Clash of Attitudes," *Washington Post National Weekly Edition*, March 25–31, 1996.

Lucy Gorham and Bennett Harrison, *Working Below the Poverty Line*. Washington, DC: The Aspen Institute, 1990.

Jacqueline Jones, *The Dispossessed.* New York: HarperCollins, 1992.

Kevin Kelly et al., "Power to the States," *Business Week*, August 7, 1995.

Robert Lavelle, ed., *America's New War on Poverty.* San Francisco: KQED Books, 1995.

Dennis McAuliffe Jr., "For Many Indian Tribes, the Buffalo Are Back," *Washington Post National Weekly Edition*, March 18–24, 1996.

Richard Morin, "Fed Up with Welfare," *Washington Post National Weekly Edition*, April 29–May 5, 1996.

Seth Mydans, "A New Wave of Immigrants on Farming's Lowest Rung," *New York Times*, August 24, 1995.

National Research Council, *Inner-City Poverty in the United States.* Washington, DC: National Academy Press, 1990.

Angela Pascopella, "Program Helps People Leave Welfare, Get Jobs," *Connecticut Post*, April 21, 1996.

Robert Pear, "House Passes an Overhaul of Welfare," *New York Times*, December 22, 1995.

Jonathan Rabinovitz, "Fighting Poverty Programs," *New York Times*, March 24, 1996.

Rochelle Ripple, "Intergenerational Education: Breaking the Downward Achievement Spiral of Teen Mothers," *Clearing House*, January/February 1994.

Eric Schlosser, "In the Strawberry Fields," *Atlantic Monthly*, November 1995.

Lisbeth Schorr, *Within Our Reach.* New York: Anchor Press, 1988.

Joseph Shapiro, "The Myths of Charity," *U.S. News & World Report*, January 16, 1995.

Ken Silverstein, "Can We Reform Welfare?" *Scholastic Update*, March 10, 1995.

Laura Summer, *Limited Access: Health Care for the Rural Poor*. Washington, DC: Center on Budget and Policy Priorities, 1991.

David Van Biema, "Can Charity Fill the Gap?" *Time*, December 4, 1995.

Barbara Vobejda, "Going Their Own Ways," *Washington Post National Weekly Edition*, February 12–18, 1996.

Edward Walsh, "Less Than a Michigan Miracle," *Washington Post National Weekly Edition*, January 1–7, 1996.

Robert White, *Tribal Assets: The Rebirth of Tribal America*. New York: Holt, 1990.

David Whitman, "Let 50 Flowers Bloom," *U.S. News & World Report*, July 3, 1995.

———, "The Myth of Welfare Reform," *U.S. News & World Report*, January 16, 1995.

# Index

# About the Author

Richard Worth has over twenty years of experience as a writer and producer for Fortune 500 clients. He has produced several hundred video presentations that run the gamut from marketing and sales programs, image pieces and training materials, to video news releases and films for corporate annual meetings. In addition he has written an eight-part radio series on Fiorello LaGuardia which aired on National Public Radio. He also presents writing seminars for corporate executives. In the textbook publishing field, he has written and edited materials in a variety of areas, including social studies, science, language arts, and health. He is also the author of nine books on topics ranging from literature to science.

# Picture Credits